THE SNOWSTORM

WRITTEN BY SELINA CHÖNZ

ILLUSTRATED BY ALOIS CARIGIET

NEW YORK

HENRY Z. WALCK, INC.

1958

This book was first published in the German language as
Der grosse Schnee, copyright 1955 by Guggenbühl & Huber, Schweizer Spiegel Verlag

First American Edition 1958

Second Printing 1960

Printed in Switzerland

Silently and softly the snow comes down,

All day and all night, on the little town;

On mountain and meadows a cold white sheet.

The poor animals can find nothing to eat.

It is as though they had been forsaken;

Only the Weather Tree stands unshaken

And spreads its limbs to shelter the outcasts

From the cold snow and icy wind blasts.

Yet it snows and snows, and all is bare,

And the animals know they won't find food there.

But Florina comes, in the gray light of day,

And they know she brings food and do not shy away.

The animals Ursli tends are quite safe and warm;
In the barn, the cattle do not care about the storm.
They lie with their young-ones on clean, dry hay,
And Ursli brings them water and food every day.
He feeds the calf its milk and brings salt to the cow.
The lamb bleats and wants to skip and play now.
Soon, the kid with the mother goat, the lambs with the sheep,
Happy and tired, fall peacefully asleep.

Ursli has tended them and watched them play;
And he leaves them now, well cared for, for the day.

He washes up, now the animals are fed,
And then goes to polish bells for his sled.
For it is nearly sledding party day,
And Ursli wants his sled to be bright and gay.
Each child paints and trims without rest
To make his be decorated best.
Each one borrows and swaps and lends,
And there's no end of fun and making friends.

In the living room, safe from the bitter weather,
The whole family is sitting together.

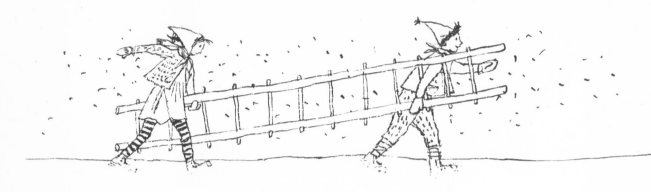

At last they run outside to the shed,
And climb up the ladder to get the sled.
Ursli says: "While I paint the sled blue,
Run to the village to the spinning-woman, who
Will give you woolen tassels—green, yellow, red.
Then ours will be the very gayest sled."
Florina complains: "It's too far to go.
I'll be cold—just look at the snow."
Ursli is cross: "How shall I decorate the sled?
It will soon stop snowing. You go ahead."

Florina cries, but she will go.
She is soon out of sight, surrounded by snow.

The spinning-woman is sweeping her floor,
When Florina knocks softly at the door.
She says hello politely and asks right away:
"Have you a bright tassel cord to make Ursli's sled gay?"
The old woman says: "I'll make it longest of all,
If you go and clean up my front hall."

The shrewd woman leaves Florina to the chore,
And Florina begins to scrub the floor.
And see – just as the hall is sparkling clean –
The most wonderful tassel cord ever seen!

Florina is pleased. "How happy Ursli will be,
When he sees all the tassels she's given me."

But now she must hurry and be on her way,
If she is to reach home while it's still day.
Florina wraps up warmly and starts to go;
The path is nearly covered up with snow.

She reaches the Weather Tree and almost goes by,
When from the shelter she hears a doe cry.
As she stops, there is a roaring, rumbling sound.
The wind whistles, and suddenly it is black all around.

Ursli is wondering at the delay
And decides he had better go meet her halfway.
He sets out to find her in the waning light.

Far from home he looks up at a terrible sight!
Down the mountainside roars a huge drift of snow.
It rages into the valley below.
Ursli cries: "Florina! Tell me where you are."
He moans: "Oh, why did I make her go so far!"
He searches on, after the avalanche,
And spies the bright cord in a broken branch.

He gropes along, with the cord as a guide.

Then he hears a faint sound – as if someone had cried.

"Florina! Florina! Hold on, it's Ursli."

And he digs and digs till he sets her free.

He grabs her, and they tremble as they look at the debris –

A jagged trunk, a branch – all that remains of the Weather Tree.

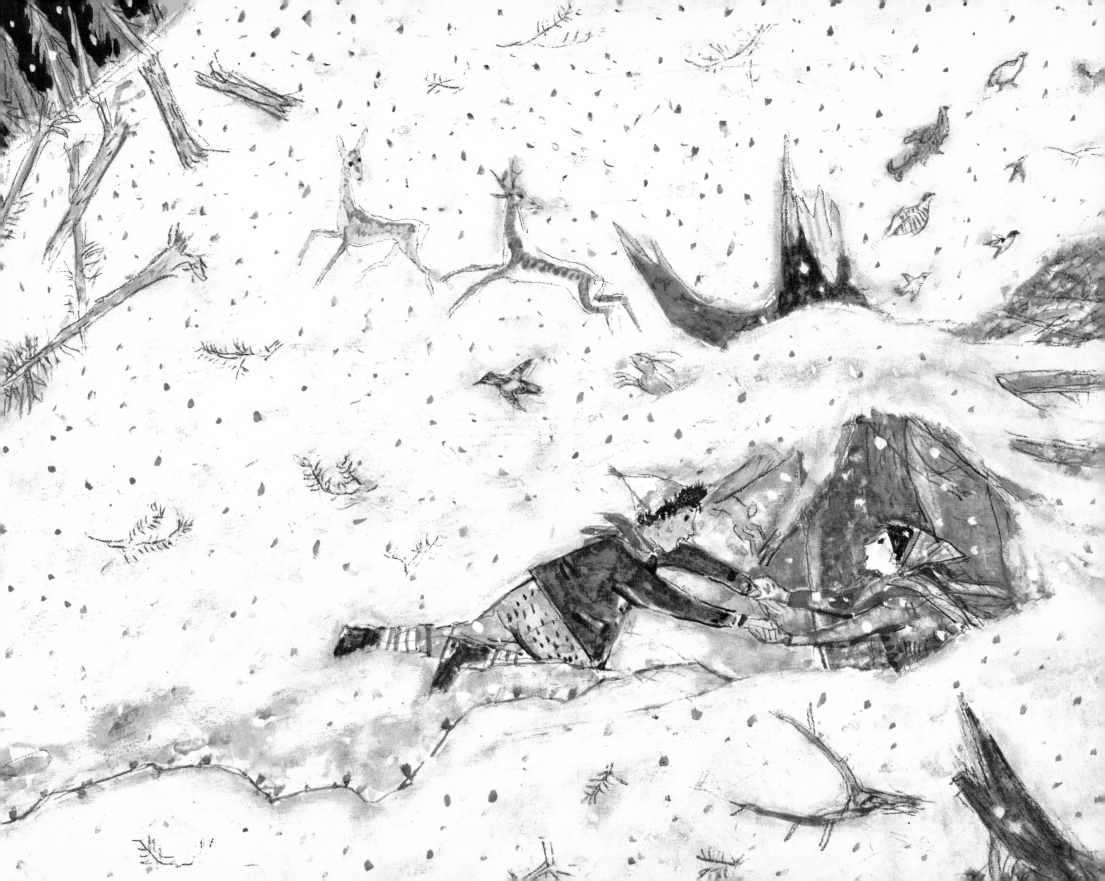

Florina sighs: "We must plant another tree
In gratitude, for it protected me."
Ursli breaks off a small limb
And takes it along home with him.

His little sister is so tired from this day
That he puts her on his back and carries her all the way.
In the dark of night they reach home once more
And steal in quietly through the back door.

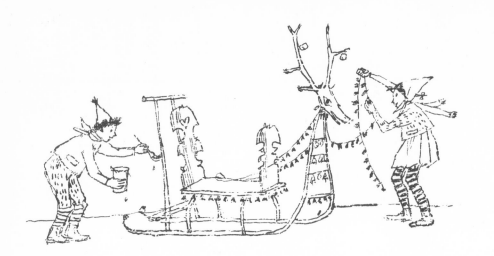

And now at last it is the day!
In a thin veil of snow the party gets under way.
Along white mountain slopes, a blue sky overhead,
Each happy child coasts on his richly trimmed sled.
When one turns over, and its riders fall out,
It is greeted with a noisy, gleeful shout.

Florina rides with Ursli, and they join in the fun.
The Weather Tree branch makes their sled the nicest one.
And many another sled is almost as gay
Because of the tassels they've given away.

And then it's the end of the lovely ride;
Everybody gathers at Ursli's fireside.
They play and dance till they're warm all through,
And they have hot chocolate and pastries, too.
Ursli plays music with his father and Uncle John,
And the children all sing, and dance on and on.

Not till the moon is shining bright,
Do they climb on their sleds and say good night.

Winter has long passed, and all the sleds
Have been stored for the summer in their sheds.

The birds that come across the sea
Must fly back and forth helplessly,
For their shelter lies ruined. Where can they go in the rain?
Will they ever find such a Weather Tree again?

Florina remembers, as she hears the birds sing,
Her wintertime pledge to plant a green sapling.
Ursli helps her, so that before long
A tree will grow there, tall and strong.